TITCH
AND
DAISY

Pat Hutchins

TITCH AND

GREENWILLOW BOOKS, NEW YORK

DAISY

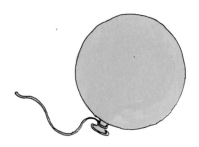

Gouache paints were used for the full-color art. The text type is Swiss 721 BT.

Copyright © 1996 by Pat Hutchins

Printed in Hong Kong by South China Printing Company (1988) Ltd.

First Edition   10 9 8 7 6 5 4 3 2 1

Library of Congress Cataloging-in-Publication Data

Hutchins, Pat (date)
Titch and Daisy / Pat Hutchins.
p.   cm.
Summary: Because he can't find Daisy at the party, Titch hides in one place after another, until finally he discovers his friend hiding because she can't find him.
ISBN 0-688-13959-0 (trade).   ISBN 0-688-13960-4 (lib. bdg.)   [1. Parties—Fiction.
2. Friendship—Fiction.]   I. Title. PZ7.H96165Tit 1996 [E]—dc20
95-2264   CIP   AC

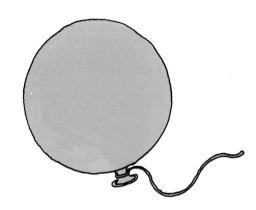

For Barbara and Henning
to read to their grandchildren

Titch didn't want to go
to the party.
"You'll make new friends,"
said Mother, "and Daisy
will be there."

Titch looked for Daisy, but
Daisy wasn't there.
"Hello," said the other children.
"Come and play with us!"
But Titch didn't want to play
if Daisy wasn't there.

He hid behind the door and watched them playing all his favorite games.
He wished Daisy were there.

"Come and dance with us!"
said the other children.
But Titch didn't want to dance
if Daisy wasn't there.

So he crept behind the sofa
and watched them dancing
all his favorite dances.
He wished Daisy were there.

"Come and sing with us!" said
the other children.
But Titch didn't want to sing
if Daisy wasn't there.

So he peeped out of the cupboard and listened to them singing all his favorite songs. He wished Daisy were there.

"Come and eat with us!" said
the other children.
But Titch didn't want to eat
if Daisy wasn't there.

He crawled under the table,
which was covered with all his
favorite things to eat.
He wished Daisy were there.

And she was.

"I hid under the table when I couldn't find you," said Daisy. "I kept wishing you were here."

"PLEASE come and eat with us,"
said the other children.
And Titch and Daisy did.

They ate all their favorite food.

And they danced,
and sang
all their favorite songs,

and played all their
favorite games,

and made lots of new friends.